Don't

Look

Back

BY

Cee McAdams

WingSpan Press

Published in the United States and the United Kingdom by WingSpan Press, Livermore, CA

The WingSpan name, logo and colophon are the trademarks of WingSpan Publishing.

ISBN 978-1-63683-019-3 (pbk.)
ISBN 978-1-63683-983-7 (ebk.)

First edition 2022

Printed in the United States of America

www.wingspanpress.com

1 2 3 4 5 6 7 8 9 10

QUOTES

"Don't look back...something might be gaining on you."
    Attributed to Satchel Paige

"Courage is the art of being the only one who knows you're scared to death."
    Earl Wilson, Quotestats.com

"The will of God will never take you where the grace of God cannot protect you."
    Mandi Merritt
    Walt Fair, PLLC

DON'T LOOK BACK

Introduction

Del 'Sling Shot' Maghenski and Al 'Bonified' Bonanavicci go way back. They have been friends since elementary school. Even though they were as opposite as a kumquat and a cherry, they were inseparable right through college. Since then, the visits have become less frequent because they live about 200 miles apart but are rarely out of touch for more than a day or so.

It had been several days since they had talked and one was worried about the other. This time it was Del who could not reach his friend so on this bright and early Saturday morning, he decided that three unanswered phone calls was reason enough to pay his friend a visit.

Del made sure that he had armed his security service, turned off all of the electrical appliances, charged his phone and packed all of the

1

Don't Look Back

essentials he would need for a weekend visit, if he stayed all weekend. He sang to himself as he readied everything for his much-anticipated trip, reminiscing about all the good times he and his friend had had over the years. With all of this packing and hurrying and anxiety, Del would forget to gas up his vehicle...and then his adventure will begin in earnest. The well-being of his friend will soon take a back seat as he weaves his way through a day filled with a bewildering, strange and sometimes terrifying set of events.

PART ONE

DON'T LOOK BACK

Del

I just can't imagine why Al's not answering the phone. It's not like him...he usually has the phone attached to his fingertips. Maybe he stepped out or is in the shower or maybe it's something else since I've been calling for 3 hours....and that's just for today...he wasn't answering yesterday and the phone went straight to voice mail...the phone wouldn't be charging this long either. I know something is amiss. Rather than continuing to guess and speculate, I'm going out there to see for myself.

It's a nice day for a long drive so I threw some things in a bag, turned on the nightlights and set the alarm. I left around 0530 hours and knew I could make this drive in under 3 hours if I didn't encounter any accidents or other traffic issues, just riding and enjoying the scenery.

Don't Look Back

Al lives close to 200 miles away but once I leave the interstate, I have to take a bit of a detour from city pavement to the dusty roads of good clean country living so it takes a bit longer, maneuvering around the little animals going about their lives, not to mention small boulders that just appear in the road with no logical explanation. Al's house was left to him by his uncle who had grown tired of the city life and wanted peace and quiet, with no sirens wailing or the sound of gunshots, nothing to scramble his nerves except the song of the tree frogs, the hoot of the owls and the nightly chorus of the cicadas. Al never shared with me what had happened to his uncle...I don't recall if the subject ever came up. The house is about a 40-minute drive from his job but he does not seem to mind.

I had been on the road for about 2 and a half hours when suddenly my Jeep Grand Cherokee developed a cough. I turned down the volume on Kenny G so that I could tune in to the noise the motor was making...it was not familiar. Suddenly it just stopped coughing, sputtered a little and then said nothing at all. I pulled over on the shoulder where it stopped on its own. Much to my chagrin, I had run out of gas. I can't imagine how I could have forgotten to get gas...well I suppose in all of my excitement and being half out of my head with worry over Al, I just didn't think to check my gas gauge...it was most certainly on empty.

I checked my surroundings to get my bearings. I had made this trip many times and knew that I was not far from Al's house, maybe a quarter of a mile or less...I also knew there was no services station close, not less than 2 miles away and it was behind me. I pondered whether to go back to get gas, call roadside assistance and wait for them to arrive or just go ahead and check on Al, then call roadside assistance...going ahead seemed like the logical thing to do...I needed to know that my friend was OK. I stepped out of the jeep, clicked the lock and started walking toward his house.

Thirty minutes later when I rounded the bend, I could see the house. It looked so tranquil and the setting was so serene it made me a bit envious... he's living out here in all of this quiet and fresh air and I live in the city in an apartment where it's never quiet. At least I know that I can come and visit whenever I like.

I walked into the yard and right away, something felt wrong. Al's front porch is wide, a semi-horseshoe with 2 rocking chairs...he is a stickler about being neat so his house is never cluttered and certainly not his front porch. There were packages and newspapers by the door and the wind had blown leaves and other debris onto the porch, not a lot, but more than he would ever tolerate. I felt a twitch and then a tickling at the base of my neck...all was not well here.

My heart began to pound and my pulse kicked up a notch. I eased up to the door and knocked...no answer. I knocked a bit louder but still no answer. I called his name but instead of him rushing out to say hello with that infectious grin on his face, I was greeted with silence. I stepped off the porch and walked around to the side of the house to see if I could get a peek into a window. I could just see through the split in the drapes but I did not understand what I saw or what I thought I had seen. There was a foot on the floor of the bedroom with the toes pointed toward the ceiling...but that can't be Al. Could he have fallen and hit his head and is he unconscious? He could not be drunk...Al does not drink to excess. I tapped on the window. No response. This was beginning to give me a bad case of the cobblywoggs!

The garage was locked so I could not determine whether or not Al's car was inside. I went around to the other side of the house to see if there was possibly a window loose that I could open but no luck. What greeted me instead was the sound of a growl, low, deep and serious. I looked up into the face of a dog the size of a llama and with canines a foot long. In my moment of fright and horror, I stumbled backward and fell...there was no time to ponder what to do next...I jumped up and ran.

I had run about 200 yards when I had to stop to catch my breath. I sat on a fallen log and reached for my phone only to discover that it was not with me. I looked around on the ground but didn't see it...I suppose I could have lost it someplace between the house and here. I patted my side where the phone is kept and realized that the holster was not with me either...I had to conclude that I had probably left them both in the Jeep. It was too far to go to get back to my car and besides, I had become somewhat disoriented out here in the forest, with all of the shadows from the tree cover. Which way was the way out and back to the interstate? I feared that I would run into that monster of a dog first, so I would just keep running in the direction that felt as if it was away from him...get lost or be attached...neither seemed like a great choice.

Reeling from the gaff of leaving my phone behind, I could only shake my head in disbelief, but in mid-shake, I heard a noise that sounded like glass breaking, more specifically, a window breaking. I

Don't Look Back

stood up and looked back in the direction of the noise; I couldn't see much but I had that unsettling feeling that that monster was racing toward me. The doors in the house were all locked so he must have jumped through a window in his search for me...my break was over...I started running faster than ever.

I remember a chat or two back when Al mentioned that he was considering adopting a shelter dog... there was no mention of taking home one of the hounds of the Baskervilles. Al having a dog and certainly one this large and terrifying definitely put a new spin on my visit...plus he didn't seem in the mood to make nice and I could not ask him what had happened to my friend...I had disturbed his peace and could only imagine him salivating, anxious to sink those 12-inch teeth into me. I ran and then ran harder, afraid to slow for fear that he would be gaining on me.

The area around Al's house is like a small forest. There are trees and vines that intertwine with the trees and form little traps for those who are not sure-footed enough to avoid them. Of course, the little animals who live here don't mind...it's just the rest of us who have intruded on their playground that can't seem to navigate the little snares, so when I tried to make a sudden turn to go around a rock, I got caught in one of them. Suddenly I was staring up at squirrels who were chattering at me. I had no time to make conversation...that dog was barreling through the forest as if the vines were not there. I got my feet underneath me, saw what appeared to be a trail and starting running as fast as I could.

In another hundred yards or so, I could see that the forest was thinning and a clearing was just ahead. I wanted to stop and listen for any traffic sounds, hoping that I was near the interstate. All I could hear was the sound of the wind in the trees...and perhaps it was only my ragged imagination, but I could hear that dog panting in between growls, still hot on my heels.

I had been running for what felt like hours. Now I had reached an area with headstones and small flower vases sitting on the ground...I had run into a cemetery. I had completely lost my sense of direction and had no clue how far away from the home of my friend I actually was...all I knew or believed I knew, was that a very large and vicious dog was pursuing me, so I just kept running...now I'm wondering if that had been the smart thing to do.

I glanced at my watch and realized that it was

Don't Look Back

nearly 10:00 hundred hours and understood why my stomach had growled at me...I was hungry...I left home rather early and had not stopped to get breakfast or even a cup of coffee, plus I was certain that I was hopelessly lost. Fatigue and despair were becoming my new buddies.

DON'T LOOK BACK

The Cemetery

Cemeteries are usually not cheery places but this one seems a bit more forlorn than most. All of the stones and monuments seemed to be leaning from sheer exhaustion of having to stand around so long. I did not want to walk through it but there seemed no way around it. I stood on the edge of it and the soil felt loamy and looked like yellow clay. It was probably only my fractured imagination but I believed that I could smell the soil, something akin to dead fish and rotting vegetation.

Al had told me a story about this area long ago when we were sitting around trading stories and lying about our college conquests. He said that long ago, this area had been a dwelling place for the native people and that his was one of their burial grounds. As with every place else, this area was invaded and forcefully taken over by the

Don't Look Back

Europeans and this cemetery has since become a resting place for those of lesser means. There is no need to wonder what lies beneath...the story as told by Al, is that sometimes on summer nights, when the moonlight shimmers in the trees, if you listen closely, you can hear the sound of chanting.

As I stood there gazing across the expanse of headstones, I just could not shake the ominous vibes this place was giving off. One of the larger monuments began to sway. I chided myself to get a grip...it was the wind and the sun and hunger pains playing tricks on my mind. Nevertheless, I moved around and away from it and tried to decide which way to go. Barely a minute had passed before another one began to sway and bow. I knew that this was illogical but I was seized with a fear that was indescribable. I began to sweat and felt as if I would lose consciousness which was the last thing I needed to do in this place.

I took a few steps to the right and felt the ground undeath my foot give away...it sank down into the loamy soil...I pulled and it came lose with a wet suction kind of sound. I took a step back... then out of nowhere, I heard a disembodied voice calling my name. I felt a jolt to my heart as if I had been hit with 200 volts of electrical power and I nearly fell. I backed up a few feet further.

Then came that voice again. I wanted to turn and run but bumped into another monument I had not noticed before. This one was taller, covered in some sort of soot and had a face that had begun to become cracked and mottled. It may have been an angel once but the wings were broken and it was so weather-beaten, that it was impossible to be sure. Now more of the monuments had joined in the chorus of calling my name and the cacophony was blended with peals of laughter and fits of sobbing, getting louder and more bizarre. I was ready to scream and run back into the forest when I felt more than saw someone walk right up to me. I was too terrified to move so I barely turned my head to see who was there...I saw no one.

Of course, it hardly seems necessary for me to state categorically that I do not believe in the supernatural...there has to be a rational explanation for what was happening but I wasted no more time trying to find one...I turned and fled back into the forest. Momentarily, I had forgotten about that humongous dog that had been chasing me.

DON'T LOOK BACK

AL & MONTEZUMA

Montezuma, Al's newly adopted shelter dog, was lying around near the body of Al without knowing what to do. Of course, Montezuma could not use the phone...all Al had was a mobile phone and it was beyond use. Montezuma had not been trained to use the phone of any sort and therefore all he could do was mourn. He did not actually know that mourning was taking place...he just thought he was anxious, hungry and a little sad... he thought that his new human dad was just taking an extremely long nap and had neglected to feed him or let him out for a bathroom break or his daily romp in the forest. Montezuma was quite fond of chewing on wood, so he missed his daily gnarring on whatever limbs he could find lying on the ground.

He was growing increasingly more agitated as

Don't Look Back

the hours passed and he became unbelievably hungry and thirsty...he had a bowl of food and water a day or was it 2 days ago, but that was long since gone. He had not been provided with a doggy door...although he was a cuddly puppy, his size would have prevented it's use anyway... so he could not escape into the backyard when bathroom breaks were necessary...in a pinch or an emergency such as now, he had to go in the corner in his room. He knew this was not part of his usual routine but his new human dad would not wake up to let him out and nature would not wait for other instructions.

When Al was first told about this little dog, it was only about 4 months old. The people at the shelter had a hard time trying to fit it into a category or decide what breed it belonged to... it was found wandering near the home of one of the shelter employees so he took it to the shelter where he worked. After a bit of work on Google, it was he who finally came to the conclusion that this puppy was a mixed breed, a combination of Caucasian sheepdog and Tibetan Mastiff or perhaps a bit of Leonberger. It was only a puppy but already quite large, about 65 pounds. By the time Al went to pick him up, he was almost the size of a Shetland.

Very early on, he showed signs of being strong-willed, intelligent and fiercely loyal...Al named him Montezuma and fell in love with him almost immediately...he just wished he would stop growing...the cost of his food was astronomical with no end in sight. Nevertheless, he grew so fond of Montezuma that he did not want to leave him home alone...he was only about 5 or 6 months old...there was no doggy daycare nearby and he could not take him to work with him, so he had no choice...Montezuma was going to have to be a latchkey puppy.

Al bought him safe toys, his own dishes and cushions in his bed to make him comfortable but Montezuma only wanted to sit or lie on Al. Al covered the outlets, removed the electrical cords and moved everything out of his reach that might crash to the floor and break...Montezuma's environment was as safe as it would have been for a human baby. Now all that was left was to be able to explain to his best friend that he has a 90-pound puppy!

Al had sent Del a picture of Montezuma when he was a much smaller ball of fur but the little puppy grew at such an alarming rate that he was already nearly 80 pounds only a week or two later. He never got the chance to show off his new furry friend to

Don't Look Back

his best buddy. Al was bending to fill Montezuma's water bowl when he felt a sharp pain that left him reeling...he dropped the water pitcher, stumbled into the bedroom, toppled over and didn't move again...he was gone. Never again would he be able to look into Montezuma's luminous brown eyes or see this big furry ton of a puppy offer so much love and demand so little. Tragedy had struck suddenly...Al was gone. Montezuma didn't know it yet but he was alone again.

MONTEZUMA

By the time Del arrived, Montezuma had been alone in the house for many hours without food or water and no human contact...he was on the grumpy side, not to mention suspicious of anyone entering or attempting to enter his home who was not familiar to him, but also excited to see someone who might let him out and play with him. He was still very much in 'guard' mode, whatever that was...he thought perhaps it meant that he was supposed to watch over his human dad and not make nice with an intruder, but when you're only a puppy and haven't learned the playbook, it's easy to get confused.

Montezuma heard the knock and immediately readied himself to spring into action...he waited to see if his human dad was going to wake up and answer the door but he still did not move. Then came the knock on the window and this made Montezuma a little nervous...this was something new. He moved from beside the bed and went to the window. There looking in at him was a new and strange human not so unlike his human dad. He tried to smile 'hello' but it was misunderstood and this new and strange person just ran away.

Montezuma paced and tried to figure out how to get out of the room so that he could go outside to meet this new person. All of the doors leading outside were closed and locked and he had not learned to open them as yet; after all, he was still a puppy-in-training...so he paced and then out of desperation, decided to jump through the window.

Montezuma sat on the ground and licked his paw...he had cut himself crashing through the window. He didn't like this new and strange sensation...he had not learned that it was called pain...he only knew that it was unpleasant and he did not like it.

After several minutes, he limped into the forest. The forest was familiar to him...it had sticks for him to gnaw and little animals to chase but today the little animals were not friendly and he was not interested in gnawing on sticks. He was hungry, thirsty and missing his human dad. Now he had this new problem...his foot hurt something awful...

the pain felt as if some cruel person had played a dastardly bad joke on him.

Montezuma finished his business and then limped on 3 legs back to his house where his human dad was still asleep and would not wake up to feed him. He limped around to the side of the house trying to find a way in but nothing doing. He knew that even with 3 good legs, he could not jump or climb back thru the window on one hurt foot, so he found a shady spot beside the house and lay down. He felt that licking his foot would bring him some comfort so he busied himself with enthusiastic licking...he was hungry, thirsty and exhausted so he finally fell asleep.

DEL

I was now caught between the leaning and bowing monuments and a vicious dog, between the proverbial rocky cliff and a bottomless pit, between a rock and a very unsettling hard place. It seemed to me that obviously these souls were not resting in peace or perhaps they sensed my presence and just wanted to chat. I had no information for them and no real interest in any they had for me so I just sat on the ground, bewildered. I think I only left home this morning but it seems as if I have been in this forest for days. I have not eaten for hours and my throat and stomach lining are dry as powder kegs. If I allow myself to think about it, I would feel desperately depressed. I left home in the early hours, with the intention of checking on my friend, which I know someplace deeply inside my soul, is not OK. Even if I had not forgotten my phone, it would do no good ... he didn't answer that anyway. I want to curl up for a nap but I don't dare. Besides that, I heard a rumble of thunder ...

Don't Look Back

rain is on the way. Getting caught out here in the rain is not my idea of a pleasure trip and I have no clue which way is out. .. I've got to get out of this forest and I have to do it before it gets dark.

Sometimes solutions to problems will just come to me if I settle down and concentrate. The mind is a strange and wonderous machine and somehow even with all of the ways we insist on twisting it, it just finds a way to get on with its business. Even with the shock of that dog leering at me through the window with those 12-inch teeth and hearing the dead call my name, I know that the signal of reason will reach me but right now, nothing is coming through. Something with a slippery feel is creeping around in the back of my head but my nerves are so badly crumpled, that I can't seem to get it to move in the right direction, toward the front so that I can make some sense of it. Maybe I'm trying too hard. I'll just sit and rest for a minute ... it will come to me.

Instead, I feel asleep. I had not intended to fall asleep. I dreamed that I was lying underneath this huge angel who keep staring down at me with malice in his eyes. It was not an angel with a kindly sweet face. It was an angel sitting in a dark corner where it got no sunshine and was covered with mold and cobwebs. It was angry that it was put in this place and blamed me for his predicament. The birds did not come to visit, only spiders and bugs up to no good.

I tried to reason with this angel and explain that I had no part in putting him where he has been placed, that I too have been put in this very dark place where I have no friends and can get food or water ... even the raindrops can't reach me. No matter what I said to him, he would not relent...he continued to be unhappy and promised to make me suffer along with him.

In the shadowy world of my dream, I grappled with the idea of a vengeful angel and began to toss and turn. Then suddenly a branch fell out of the tree. Somewhere above me, someone was shaking me and startled me awake. I jumped to my feet, realizing that it has begun to rain. I also realized that after all of this time, that dog would have had a chance to find me and he was nowhere in sight. Could this be that slippery thought that has refused to attach itself to one of the only active brain cells I have at the moment? Where is the dog and why has it not continued to hunt for me? And who is this person standing before me?

He was saying to me that he had been calling my name for quite some time and got no response.

Don't Look Back

He had seen me standing around at the edge of the cemetery and he wondered whether or not I was loss or having some type of breakdown. He was explaining to me that he lived not far over the rise and could just make out that someone was over here and appeared to be in trouble ... he wondered if he could help.

For a moment, I felt the ground underneath my feet tilt a bit...I staggered backward and leaned against the tree ... finally, the fog began to lift and I turned to the face this stranger. He was a big guy with a scruffy beard and kind eyes. He was dressed in coveralls of some description, a bit dirty and worn at the knees, the standard garb of farmers ... we were both getting soaked to the skin so I think he must have been anxious to get someplace out of the rain.

He asked my name but I'm not sure how I responded .. .! just nodded and tried to smile. He was speaking to me again but I kept tuning out and missed most of what he was saying. Finally, he put his hand on my shoulder and asked if I wanted to come home with him ... it was a bit of a long walk, not too fancy but warm and dry inside. I nodded dumbly and started walking with him.

Now that it was raining harder and the clouds

were hanging low, I could no longer see the sun .. .in the overcast sky, I was unable to discern the position of the sun or which direction we were walking ... all I was able to determine was that we were leaving the cemetery with the leaning monuments. I could blame my parents for not making me a boy scout when I was much younger but that would hardly help me at this point. .. I will just have to follow my new friend and hope that he will help me find the interstate so that I can get back to my Jeep .. .I need to check on Al.

When we reached his house, he opened the door for me and offered me a seat at his table. He walked over to a cabinet and took out 2 glasses which he proceeded to fill with a warm brown liquid. He handed one to me and took one for himself. Not wanting to offend my new friend, I tossed mine down with one swallow. Suddenly I felt my head do a crazy whirligig and my stomach turn upside down ... then it was hopelessly on fire and not an ice cube in sight.

While I was doing a slow burn, my friend was busy stirring something in a cast iron pot... I couldn't see what it was but it smelled like a combination of a male locker room and burned bacon. Then he was filling a bowl and handing it to me. My brain was still in disconnect status ...

Don't Look Back

after all, I had been having a conversation with cemetery monuments ... otherwise, I would have graciously refused it but my brain and stomach were not on the same page so I accepted it and began to spoon it into my mouth as if it were the world's best cuisine.

Conversation was light as we enjoyed our lunch ...in fact, we hardly spoke. I glanced around at my friend's place at the part that must have been the kitchen. There were small gaps in the wall, nothing large enough to emit an animal the size of a raccoon but large enough for any number of critters that creep, crawl or slither. I could tell that he had tried to cover some holes with thin sheet metal but I suspect that it will not do much to staunch the hefty winter temps. I managed to stop chewing long enough to ask if he could show me how to get back to the interstate where I had left my Jeep. I told him that my friend lived somewhere nearby and I needed to get gas so that I could go to his house and check on him.

After we finished the soup or whatever it was called, my new friend offered to help me get out of the forest and back to the interstate, providing that his truck would start. We went out to the barn and without too much effort, the truck started. He gave it a little too much gas and it coughed and smoked a bit but otherwise kept running.

I climbed into the seat beside him and struggled not to shiver, still wet from being in the rain .... my sodden clothes were mostly stuck to me but I was no longer starving and tried to pretend that I felt daisy-fresh.

DON'T LOOK BACK

Mailman

Sometime in the afternoon, Montezuma was awakened by the sound a vehicle approaching... it was the mail carrier. Montezuma had heard this vehicle many times but had only seen or sniffed the mailman through the door...now he saw him driving up to the house. Montezuma struggled up on his 3 good legs, and hobbled over to the vehicle. The mailman saw him approaching but did not dare get out of his vehicle...he saw this humongous dog coming toward him that seemed to be limping and thought it a bit odd . Usually, he would just leave the mail on the front porch if there were large envelops or packages that were too large for the box but today, he had only small envelops and had no reason to get out anyway. However, he was astonished at the sight of this very large dog...he had only caught a glimpse of him a few weeks back and he did not seem this large. He wondered out loud what kind of dog this was and why it was allowed to be outside... he knew that Al would not just leave him out or at least he had not done this before.

This little animal was limping badly, obviously in physical distress; now the mailman looked around and discovered that the window had been broken and that there was glass on the ground. He wanted to go up to the door and knock but was terrified of this very large dog. He stared at the dog and the dog stared right back with those soulful luminous brown eyes. He wasn't snarling or barking...he just appeared to be in great pain. The mailman knew it was not a good idea to interact with the dogs on his route and decided that the right thing to do was to leave and call the animal control and let them investigate.

He left the mail in the box and drove back down the driveway. He was nearing the end of his route and was anxious to get home...the following Monday was a holiday and he had big plans. He decided that he would wait until he was done delivering the mail and then he would make the call to animal control.

The mailman stopped at his last address, the home of a friend, and spent more time than usual chatting. Sometime during the conversation, he remembered the very large dog that he had seen in Al's yard. The neighbor, who lived about a half mile from Al's house, had not visited Al for several days and had not seen the dog, but now that the mailman was so excited about him, he thought it best that he go and get a look at this monster of a dog... but first he would call animal control...just in case the dog was vicious or something worse.

By the time the neighbor arrived at Al's house, animal control was already there and had captured the dog. One of the technicians explained to him that the dog, although very large, was only a puppy. He had been hurt, most likely from jumping through the window, and may have been several days without food. He said that he had knocked on the door and had called out to Al but had gotten no response...the doors were all locked but through the one of the windows, they could see what appeared to be a person lying on the floor. The local constabulary had been notified and was on his way. They wanted to wait for him before they took the dog away.

The Sherriff's deputy arrived shortly thereafter and pulled to a stop in the driveway. He got out of his vehicle, hitching up his pants, weighed down by an equipment belt loaded with a large weapon and stuff that seemed unnecessary. He asked the obligatory questions: did we touch anything? Had we been inside? And so forth. No, we had not been inside and the only thing we touched was this very large hungry puppy who would like us to feed him and give him some water.

He walked up to the door and knocked. No response. He called out to identify himself but still no response. He tried the knob but the door was locked. He then proceeded to checked around the sides of the house and found that a window had been broken from the inside out. We told him it was this way when we arrived and we believe that this was how the dog had gotten out and how he had sustained the injury to his paw.

The deputy looked through the broken window and saw a foot with the toes pointed up...he stuck his head inside and was immediately assaulted by the smell...he did not enter but went back to his vehicle to call the wagon...the deputy had found Al.

MONTEZUMA

Montezuma had now been captured a second time in his very young life and taken to a strange place, only this time he was old enough to remember that he once had a home and a human dad. He had been given food and water and some kind person had fixed his paw so that he was no longer in pain, at least not so much. Now he just wanted to go home and play with his human dad and cuddle up in his very own bed. Unfortunately, this was not to be, at least not just yet.

Everyone gathered around and admired him and wondered what kind of dog he was ... the vet or whomever had fixed his paw, said he would be interested in keeping him if no one came to claim him. Montezuma just wanted to take a nap if he could not go home. Instead, he was put inside a large cage and left in a poorly lit alcove ... this certainly did not feel like his home ... the only good thing was he had treats and a nice cool bowl of water ... he thought he could just be content for now. As soon as his foot was well, he would go home to his human dad and his real house.

THE FARMER

My new friend, the farmer, had taken me to the service station to buy enough gas to get me started then I made a return trip to fill up. I was thrilled beyond description to see my Jeep, where it sat looking forlorn but otherwise untouched except by a few drops of rain. By the time I made it back to Al's house, darkness was slowly creeping in...my new friend the farmer had left me at the service station so he was not around to lend me his hand for support. I forced myself to dredge up the last of my courage and stepped out of my Jeep.

The first thing I noticed was the broken window and the glass on the ground. I faintly remember hearing glass breaking so many hours ago when I felt certain that enormous dog was hot on my heels. Now there was no sign of the dog. If he were anywhere around, he would have greeted me by now, but just in case, I stood very still and did not move far away my Jeep. I honked the horn, one short blast but still nothing or no one came forward.

I felt that cold wind creeping past my ears again, and the blood began to sizzle in my veins, kind of a humming, water-rushing feeling, when you know something is not quite right but words or explanations elude you. I waited another minute and then walked slowly up to the door and knocked. No answer. I decided to try the door knob...it turned in my hand. I pushed the door open one centimeter at a time. I was standing in the front room; it smelled faintly of dog and dry leaves...a house that has been closed for several days would probably smell this way...I had no way of knowing how long Al had been away. I call out to him...no response...my nerves began to jangle and the temperature of that cold wind dropped a few degrees.

Cautiously, I proceeded forward, shivering from the cold sensation as if I had just survived colliding with a semi...I decided to go and check out the room where the window was broken, which would be Al's bedroom. I saw no sign of the dog or Al... the bed was still made, but a board had been placed over the bottom of the window. This was all very strange.

I took a few minutes and looked around the house, what Al had referred to as his cabin in the woods. I saw the dog's bed, bowls and toys in that one small room that would have been an office, if Al had chosen to use it as such, but he had apparently converted it into the room for the dog...I took note but did not make a close examination. I walked around, checking in other spaces, the guest bedroom, but found no sign that Al had had company recently and there were no dirty dishes in his sink...but this was not a surprise. There were no notes or anything to indicate where he had gone or when he would return.

I have been here many times, but now it feels different. I can almost feel a presence but not Al's...the house was without its warmth and I feel oddly like an intruder...it was time to leave.

On my way out, I noticed that the lock had been forced and a small note stuck just to the side of the door...I had missed it on my way in. My pulse kicked up a notch as I retrieved the note with shaky fingers and sweaty palms...it stated simply 'whomever finds this note, call the sheriff's office.' My heart sank as I realized, without a doubt, that something bad had definitely happened to my friend.

DON'T LOOK BACK

Part Two

Don't Look Back

Montezuma was in this place with many other animals, some barking and whining and making sounds that he had long ago left behind, when his new human dad had come to take him home. Now he wondered why he was here again, and what had happened to his human dad...he wondered if he was still taking his really long nap...he must have been really sleepy.

DON'T LOOK BACK

After speaking to the sheriff's deputy on the phone, I headed for the office, driving too fast. It was a deep and profound message that the deputy was trying to pass on but he seemed reluctant to hit me over the head with it. Nevertheless, I was expecting the worse as I roared into the parking lot, my pulse pounding...I felt something akin to an adrenaline rush but nothing short of agony.

The deputy looked at me as if I were his child who had disappointed him. He shifted uncomfortably in his chair, expelled a long breath he seemed to have been holding all day. He thanked me for calling after finding his note. He said this would seem like the wrong time but this is the only time that we would have, then proceeded to speak in a rather official manner.

I tried to listen to the deputy but he seemed a million miles away. He was talking about how they had found Al and had removed the puppy from the premises, the condition of the house and something about the next of kin would have to be notified...I tuned out, then something he said made me tune in again...did he just say they took Al's puppy away? I was remembering the last conversation I had with my friend...had he mentioned a puppy? Could it have been the same dog I saw through the window at Al's house, that humongous dog that had chased me through the forest? Or did I only think that it had been chasing me? I don't remember Al telling me about a ferocious one-ton puppy! That little bit of information must have gotten lost among the jokes and talk of all of the good times we had...it all seems so long ago now.

I was not ready to accept that he was gone. I forced myself to blink back tears. I wanted to rush out of the building so that I could scream into the clouds but knew I needed to know what had happened, but the deputy could only tell me as much as he was allowed, then directed me to other offices and other people.

I went back to my jeep and sat in silence. I didn't want stay in this place, but I didn't want to leave, go home and think about coming back another day...I didn't exactly know what to do. I was not the next of kin and had no authority to make decisions about what to do about Al...I wasn't even sure they would allow me to see him one last time or give me any information about what had happened to him...I decided to try...it was the least I could do...then I would make that much dreaded call to his parents.

I drove to yet another official looking building and sat before yet another seriously official person. My throat felt dry and parched and I was afraid that I would make a croaking sound if I tried to speak. There was a knot in my stomach the size of Vermont, a combination of hunger, anxiety and dread. I swallowed hard just for something to do and waited for this guy to speak.

He was using some of the same words as the deputy, words and phrases no doubt practiced just for occasions such as this. He was saying that he only had a preliminary report and could only give me a short version of that since I was not the next of kin but could I please be kind enough to make the identification. I nodded like a mindless bobble-head and followed him

Don't Look Back

through a series of double doors into a very cold room, but made it no further...there was a sudden whirlwind in my stomach and my knees turned into jello...I was suddenly outside in the corridor, leaning against the wall, examining the floor. Someone was speaking to me again but I had tuned out...the only word I thought I had heard was 'aneurism' but at that moment, it did not register.

This official in a long white jacket was still speaking but I straightened up, stood on shaky knees, thanked him for his time and told him that I would return as soon as Al's parents arrived... then I left the building. I had almost forgotten about Al's puppy...I would have to find out about him on another day...I drove home in a fog with a very heavy heart.

I crawled out of my jeep, stalked up to my apartment and let myself inside. It was dark, silent and oppressive. It felt as if I had been gone for a year but it had only been one day. I have not yet come to the full realization of just how much the death of Al has affected me...I know that it is deep and profound but it has affected me in other areas of my life that I prefer to ignore at this moment in time.

The signs that I am missing him are everywhere...I made a tall drink and prepared to sit by the window and have this long discussion with him about yesterday's world events with a sprinkling of our usual 'old buddy' nonsense, as it was our usual custom...I had actually hit speed dial, waited for his number to connect, before realizing that he was not going to answer. I feel an utter loneliness...death has invaded my life...it came unannounced and uninvited and has whisked Al away. I suppose Death does not owe it to us to be polite and courteous, make an appointment or even send a text message...he just shows up, takes whatever or whomever he wants, then departs... such is the power of Death. I stood, went to the sink and dumped out the drink. I will have to find another time to deal with my grief.

I hope that at some point in time, I can find some respite in a deep, dreamless sleep. I'm afraid to dream...I know Al will be there and he will ask why I had let him down, why I had not gone to see about him sooner...I will have no answers. The heaviness of my grief over-took me and I passed out cold.

I came awake with a start, not sure at first what the noise was, a jangling or something...then realized that it was the phone. I tried to hurry to answer but dropped it several times before getting a grip and saying hello. Al's dad was speaking, saying that they were taking the next flight out to go and pick up their son so that they could take him home for burial, a 2-hour flight and could I meet them at Al's house...there were things they needed to discuss with me...I assured him that I would be there.

I bumped into the wall a few times before I finally found the shower, then let the cold water do its job of clearing the cobwebs and getting the oxygen flowing. I felt as if I had been on a long bender and was trying to sober up before the next AA meeting. By the time I got out of the shower, I felt almost human. I hurriedly dressed and made a note to myself to be sure to stop for coffee and gas before I hit the interstate.

I sat and watched the tears slowly and silently glide down the cheeks of Al's mother and watched as his father gently tried to comfort her. I can only imagine what it's like to lose a child, this deep and extraordinary relationship that has been severed...surely this bond between mother and child that can never be broken but the pain must be unbearable.

They wanted to know if I were here with Al when this tragedy happened...they were hoping that he was not alone. Sadly, I had to admit that I was not and that it had taken 3 unanswered calls before I came to see why he wasn't responding...he was apparently already gone when I arrived.

Eventually the conversation turned to the subject of Al's puppy and what had to be done about him. I recounted my first impression of him and that made them smile. However, according to the sheriff's deputy, this very large dog is only a puppy, just a few months old. Al's dad remembered him saying something about adopting a shelter dog but they never knew what breed or size or any other details about him...nevertheless, it is Al's dog and they could not take him home with them on the plane so would I take him and give him a home...and why not stay here where he is already comfortable...we could talk later about a more permanent arrangement for the house.

My scalp began to itch in strange places as I remembered the face of what I considered a vicious beast, even thought he had chased me into the forest...now they were asking me to take him in and make him my very own pet? I gave voice to my thoughts and they both shrugged and waved off my doubts, stating that it was all a part of that moment of queasiness, wondering if you can be devoted to something else other than your own pleasures...they assured me that it would pass and that I would grow to love the little animal...(That was hardly a little animal I saw in that window!) So as not to bring any more worry or stress on Al's parents, I promised to do my best to give the puppy good care...hopefully, love would come later...thankfully they could not hear the bangs and yowls of my heart, fear that I would become the little animal's next meal.

We exchanged hugs and off they went to get their son for his trip home...they told me that they would arrange to have his vehicle picked up later...dad may even come and drive it back. I locked the door as Al and I had exchanged keys long ago, but in my state of extreme anxiety and fright, I had forgotten that the key was on my keyring. I took one look around and knew that I was going to take them up on their offer to live here...I would forever feel close to Al and besides, my apartment was no place for a dog, especially not one this size. So why do I feel as if I just booked passage on the Titanic?

All the way back to my apartment, I thought about having to live with this gigantic dog, Al's orphan puppy. I had promised his mom and dad so there was no getting around it...it was a scary thought and more than a little terror coursed through my veins...the very idea was giving me a case of the cobblywoggs, sort of like walking into a tunnel blindfolded!

My lease was not going to be up for another 2 months but I knew I could not wait that long to pick up the puppy – no telling what would happen to him in that time. However, there were all manner of chores that I had to attend to before leaving, not the least of which was to notify my place of employment...I was surely going to have to find a job closer to Al's house. I sent my boss an email explaining the new development and requested some time off to get the situation under control. Not five minutes later, my boss called, expressing his condolences and his total disbelief...yes it was awful about Al and yes take as much time as I needed...he would see what he could do about a transfer and yes, I could count on him for an exceptional recommendation if it came to that but let's hope not. When he hung up, I breathed a heavy sign of relief!

The people at the city pound were not especially happy to see me, especially after I told them I was there to pick up Al's puppy...someone there had decided to claim him and hoping no one showed up in the next day or so...truthfully, I was more than a little nervous to finally come face to face with the dog I had seen through that window, puppy or not.

I was told to wait and that they would bring the dog out to me...not to worry...he is a friendly sort, but he is awfully large. I did not give a voice to my thoughts but I stood near the door, just in case. Momentarily the dog came through the door, literally dragging the attendant along. He was wearing a collar with the initial M on it...no one seemed to know what it meant...no worries, I mused...I'm sure to figure it out sooner or later.

When he walked up to me, he was up to my knees, as large as a fully grown German Shepard, with a fierce look in his eyes and much more fur. He sniffed my fingers and legs and did not find me objectionable so I relaxed only a hair. I inquired when he had eaten last and was told about an hour before I arrived...my pulse ticked down another notch...perhaps I would not be his lunch after all. They handed me a document to sign, the leash was removed and we were ready to leave.

The puppy followed me out to my jeep, climbed into the back without assistance and off we went, back to his home, only without his former dad... how he would respond to me in the coming days was a mystery, a mystery no one more eager to solve than me. As soon as we reached the driveway, he started dancing, happy and excited to be home. I opened the back and he bounded out and into the forest...I realized that they had forgotten to give me a leash.

I began my first day in my new house by walking around, trying to get acclimated...I had cleaned up the dog's room and had called someone to come and replace the broken window but now I opened all of the windows to let some fresh air in... something new to me since life in an apartment in the city does not allow for this kind of getting up close to nature. I stored most of my things in the spare bedroom, got some fresh linen and re-made the bed, just so the house would feel more like I actually lived here. I don't plan to change much, at least not for a while...I think I want to feel as if Al is still here...I know I'm having a bit of a delusionary episode but hopefully it will pass.

It had not taken long to discover that the M on the dog's collar stood for Montezuma...it was stenciled on his bowls and written on the pillow on his bed. I thought Montezuma was an interesting choice of name! I will have to do more research to see who exactly Montezuma was, man or beast, fierce warrior or a ballistic fur ball.

Before nightfall, he took me for a run through the forest [again] and introduced me to his favorite trees. The attendant has said that he had a cut on his paw but I saw no signs of it bothering him as he ran through the house and certainly not while watching him race through the grass and around the trees. He has obviously grown more because he was now up to my thighs and probably weighs more than me.

Nighttime comes early here among all of these trees or seems to here in this new place...I felt a bit out of sync so I tried to busy myself with gathering up Al's things for his parents...I soon grew depressed and went to bed after making sure that Montezuma was all tucked in for the night...or so I thought.

No sooner had I fallen into a deep sleep did I feel or hear something moving, curtains being drawn, heavy objects being dragged across the floor and rapping sounds. I sat bolt-upright, looked around but saw nothing out of the ordinary...of course I had no clue what the ordinary was here...perhaps this happened all the time. I must have made a noise because the dog came into the room and jumped

Don't Look Back

on the bed...my heart nearly stopped, starring into those luminous brown eyes, thinking he was about to rip out my throat...instead he whined and lay down beside me, almost on top of me in a protective gesture. I rubbed his head and told him it was OK, too afraid to ask him to get down from the bed...actually, it was somewhat comforting, knowing something this big was on my side. I lay back down and tried to get back to sleep.

Instead, I lay in bed, starring up at the ceiling, with the dog lying beside me. I could not will myself to sleep but did close my eyes, hoping it would help the anxiety to dissipate and in short order, surprisingly I fell asleep. Again I was awaken by sounds of the night, the house letting me know that it was alive, whether or not it was to my liking. I had no recollection of any foreign feelings, no feeling of not being welcomed or wanted, when I entered Al's house, recently or on any other occasion. I did not walk into this house with a feeling that I had interrupted patterns or rituals because these things would be alien to me anyway. Now I have the sense that this house was accustomed to the habits and behavior of its former occupants and perhaps I should not stay... or my mind is playing tricks on me, knowing that something tragic happened here to someone really close to me and perhaps my guilt is tainting my imagination.

Exhaustion took over and I finally fell into a fitful sleep, not resting but tossing and turning until morning. Montezuma was nudging my face, wanting to go out so I had to be up before I wanted to be, feeling as if I had gone 5 rounds with the Masked Marauder. I threw on a bathrobe and let him out to do his run into the forest. I had discovered that he had a penchant for gnawing on sticks, not just any stick would do, but he was quite selective about the stick he chose to chew, which I found to be interesting. When he was done, we went into the house to find breakfast... his was already prepared...I just had to find something for myself.

I did not find the kitchen too well stocked, cereal mostly, not bagels or cheese or any kind of fruit and knew I would have to make a trip to the supermarket soon, wherever that was. Montezuma could probably show me the way.

Don't Look Back

Over the next several nights, the visits from the unknown entity continued. I would be awakened by hands shaking me but there would be no one there. Cold hands would touch my face but I never saw anything more than a shadow...one night, the light in the kitchen came on but only for a nano second, then went off before my eyes could convince my mind that it really happened. These mysterious and unsettling visits became increasingly more terrifying and continued until one night, I decided to stay up and wait for whomever or whatever was intent on keeping me awake, a thin line between desperation and insanity.

I am not a believer in curses or ghosts or any kind of other-worldly entities but rather believe that there is a logical explanation for things, no matter how bizarre they may appear at the time. Al and I never made it a habit to discuss this kind of phenomena nor did I grow up listening to ghost stories as told by my parents or grandparents as their way of either amusing themselves or preserving some snippet of old family history. Whatever is taking place in this house, Al's house, is not so much in conflict with my true beliefs, but more like I've stepped into a puddle of some else's traumatic history...or maybe it's something else entirely.

I sat by the window, night after night and watched as the moon passed over the trees. The night looked somehow menacing, shadows dancing and twirling in every direction, and I had the uncanny feeling of being watched... then morning would come and the day would begin again. Montezuma and I had settled into an easy routine...he grew bigger, ate a lot more and one day I realized that Al's dad had been correct...I had grown to love this enormous dog...he was now my large baby and I was his new dad...I had gotten past the fear of becoming his next meal and did more worrying about him than me...it happened without any unusual effort on my part. Whatever inexplicable things are happening in this house, we are going to deal with them together.

I had taken a nap early in the day, preparing for my all-night vigil at the window. Tonight I hoped to meet this entity, to discuss our issues, perhaps have a midnight snack together. I sat down to wait...I did not have to wait too long.

First there was a rattling and then a groan, then the room became eerily dark, cold and silent, the silence almost deafening. The room felt as if it was filling up with very cold air, as if the air conditioner had clicked down 40 degrees all my itself. Floor boards began to creak that had not creaked before...I could feel a presence but nothing moved and neither of us spoke. Despite the cold temperature of the room, I began to sweat. I wondered where was Montezuma...I could use the comfort of his warm fur.

The room changed from very dark to a kind of blue aura, like blue-tinted fog with spiderwebs. Out of the fog, an apparition began to form, with arms that looked more like broken angel's wings, a spectre out of some long ago nearly forgotten nightmare...it looked vaguely familiar but in my state of mind, I could not remember why. I wished at that moment that I could transform myself into Harry Houdini and be miles away in seconds but no such luck. This entity held me in its macabre grasp without a touch or a word. I lost touch with time, space and consciousness.

Then the sun was streaming through the window, and Montezuma was there, wanting to go out. It took me a moment to round up my faculties and get them all lined up...I felt slightly dizzy, as if I had been inhaling too much incense. I was still sitting there by the window, the snack untouched. Without being able to conjure up an explanation, rational or otherwise, I stumbled out of the door with Montezuma for his morning run.

When I made it back inside, the phone was ringing...my boss was on the line informing me that I would need to return to work, that he was unable to facilitate a transfer, but that a position had opened up that would mean a raise in pay. I told him that I appreciated his efforts and that I would get back as quickly as possible.

I contacted the old apartment management to inquire about a pet-friendly apartment and they had one available in another building not far away from where I worked, but not one where I was before. Details were worked out and I was going to be able to move in right away. This unhappy house with its restless and disgruntled inhabitants will have to get along without Montezuma and me.

I called Al's dad to see when he could come to pick up Al's vehicle and he told me he could do it right away...he didn't realize there was a need to hurry...he wanted to know why I had decided not to stay and I told him simply that it was too far from my job...I left out the visits from the cold, unfriendly night visitors.

I met him at the airport, drove him to the house and he collected Al's vehicle and other personal belongings. He told me that he would later contact a real estate agent to see about selling the property since I had decided not to live there. He was not immensely excited to meet Montezuma, the former grand-dog so their good-bye was a simple wave and he was gone.

All of the arrangements had been made and the date for Al's memorial service had been set. I promised his parents that I would take an early flight so that I could be there to help as much as I was needed. Montezuma was anxious, and seemed to know that I was going away and leaving him behind. Each time I left the room, he was hot on my heels. I had bought him all manner of sticks and other chew toys but nothing was of interest to him today except me. When I opened the door for him to go out, he promptly sat and stared at me. I knew what he was feeling...I could sense his fear of being abandoned but there was no choice...I could not take him with me.

I had promised my boss that I would only be gone for one more day and then I would work all the overtime needed to get caught up and back on track. My boss is somewhat unflappable and told me that there was no need for promises...just go and bid farewell to my friend and let tomorrow take care of itself.

The service was somber, as one would expect, short but dignified. I sat beside Al's mom and she seemed to appreciate that she had an extra pair of arms for comfort. The chapel was packed with mourners, some of them I remembered from long ago, when Al and I were much younger. His dad was mostly stoic and people would pass by and smile but he seemed to acknowledge no one... grief can seem like a very cowardly but sometimes jealous companion.

Don't Look Back

One morning as I was reading the paper, I saw an article which made my eyebrows bounce up and down. Al's cabin in the woods had been sold weeks ago but the new owners had not stayed there more than a few days. They told the reporter that they kept hearing strange noises that kept them awake at night. At first, they would go to bed with all of the lights on in the house but that didn't work well at all...they plugged in nightlights...they left candles burning...out of desperation, they installed lights around the outside of the house...no matter what they tried, the noises continued. Some nights, the lights would be turned off or the candles blown out. Finally, they had had enough...they called the realtor and put the house up for sale.

Weeks have now gone by and still no takers. Potential buyers had heard the stories and would politely decline. Several investors expressed an interest in buying the property but decided that they could not turn a profit if no one wanted to stay there, not even for one night.

It would have been hard or impossible for me to understand and believe the stories associated with this house had I not experienced the unbelievable for myself. There is actually no evidence of any murders or any other kind of horrible event that took place within those walls...just the tragic death of a friend gone way too soon. Perhaps that malevolent spirit traipsing through the house on his nightly forays, was simply lost and wanted help finding his way to his forever resting place, and became increasingly more agitated with my continued failure to comprehend. Although I wish him success in finding his way, I'm happy to admit that I resigned as the incompetent navigator.

Al's little once bucolic cabin in the woods has now fallen into disrepair and slow decay. What was once a place of joy is now a thing of ruin. I wonder if there were messages that the previous occupants, including me had simply failed to correctly interpret...I wonder if there were messages from the leaning and bowing monuments, and that

Don't Look Back

under the invisible weight of fear, I was simply unable to understand.

The memory of those nights still lingers, and sometimes still causes my pulse to rachet up a notch or two. Tonight as I lay and listen to the rain, it all seems so long ago. The night was quiet and peaceful and I soon drifted into untroubled sleep.

When I awoke later, the moonlight was just peeking through the clouds. I stood at the window and listened to the sounds of the night. Standing next to me was Montezuma, my gentle giant, now fully grown and weighing about 160 pounds...he grew up so fast!

WEDDING DAY

Love Celebrated

Hopes & Dreams Realized

Happiness in Bloom

cancelled

THE WEDDING

The music is playing...I'm ready to dance but
I don't feel a cheek...champagne is chilled and
the mood is right...there's no one here but me...
I lift my glass to sip a toast...not a person was
speaking...not even a ghost...the tables were set
with napkins and care...no food no drink no cake
was there...I wanted to talk to my guests and the
groom...the silence was deafening inside this
room...the doorbell is ringing, the guests finally
here...I ran to the door but no one was there...
the lawn had been cut, the flowers arranged...
the chairs decorated with ribbons and things...
my imagination has faulted again...I'm afraid that
Covid cancelled all my plans.

Cee McAdams

www.ingramcontent.com/pod-product-compliance
Lightning Source LLC
Chambersburg PA
CBHW030540180626
46810CB00005B/1948